Toby

story by MARGARET WILD · pictures by NOELA YOUNG

TICKNOR & FIELDS *Books for Young Readers*

New York 1994

First American edition 1994 published by
Ticknor & Fields
Books for Young Readers
A Houghton Mifflin company, 215 Park Avenue South,
New York, New York 10003.

First published in Australia by Omnibus Books

Manufactured in the United States of America

Typography by David Saylor
The text of this book is set in 18 point Kennerly
The illustrations are watercolor reproduced in full color

HOR   10 9 8 7 6 5 4 3 2 1

Library of Congress Cataloging-in-Publication Data

Wild, Margaret.
Toby / written by Margaret Wild : illustrated by Noela Young.—
1st American ed.
p. cm.
Summary: When Toby the dog gets old and sick and finally dies,
the children who love him express their love in different ways.
ISBN 0-395-67024-1
[1. Death–Fiction. 2. Dogs–Fiction.] I. Young, Noela, ill.
II. Title.
PZ7.W64574To 1994
[E]—dc20
93-14394   CIP   AC

For the Doyle children, who loved their old Gough
—M. W.

For Kay and Kim, and for Walter always
—N. Y.

OUR dog Toby is fourteen. That's pretty old for a dog.
My little brother Ben wants him to live until he's thirty,
so he can be in *The Guinness Book of Records*. "You'll be
famous," he tells Toby. "Famous!"

Toby is really my big sister Sara's dog. She's nearly twelve. Mom says that when Sara was a baby, she would climb all over Toby and pull his ears and dress him up and fall asleep next to him.

When Sara started school, Toby would follow her every day and wait by the gate until school let out.

And every Saturday Sara and Toby would go to the park and whiz faster, faster on the merry-go-round.

Then Sara would throw the tennis ball, again and again, and Toby would keep bringing it back, all drippy with spit, until they were both so tired they'd just flop on the grass and look up at the sky.

But Toby doesn't wait for Sara at the school gate anymore. He doesn't go for walks, and he just blinks his eyes when she throws the ball and says, "Fetch, boy, fetch!"

Sara hurls the ball into the bushes and screams, "What's the matter with you, you stupid old dog!"

Sometimes Maree from next door looks over the fence
at Toby. She says very loudly, "That dog is old and sick.
You should call the vet."

Toby heaves himself up and wags his tail. He barks
playfully at Maree and brings us the tennis ball.
"Good," says Maree, "there's life in the old dog yet," and
she goes back to taking the washing off the line.

But Toby doesn't stay perky for long. We know he's old and sick. He's also a little blind and a little deaf, and he often makes such bad smells that everyone shouts and leaps for the window.

Of course we all forgive him, all except Sara. She walks around with her hand over her nose.

And when Toby puts his head on her knee, she pushes him off and says, "You're old and smelly. Go away." She stares at Toby with angry, sad eyes, then jumps up and goes to her bedroom and slams the door.

Ben is furious. "I hate Sara," he says. "Why is she so mean to Toby? He can't help being old and smelly."

Mom tries to explain. "Everything is changing for Sara," she says. "Next year she starts junior high school, and that means catching two buses and making new friends."

"So?" says Ben. He wouldn't care if he had to catch a zillion buses and make loads of new friends.

Mom goes on. "Sara's growing up, and she's not sure that she likes it."

"So?" says Ben again. I bet he wishes he would grow up. If he had muscles and a mustache, no one would be able to push him around.

"So," says Mom, "Sara doesn't want anything else to change. She doesn't want Toby to get old and die. She wants him to stay just the way he always was. She still loves him, you know."

"Ha!" says Ben. "Ha!"
I know just how he feels.

So Ben and I look after Toby. We feed him and bathe him and shoo away the flies.

And on Saturdays we put him in the old baby carriage and take him for a walk in the park.

Toby is so weak now he can hardly move. On Tuesday, when Maree puts her head over the fence and says as usual, "That dog is old and sick. You should call the vet," he just shuts his eyes and goes back to sleep.

Maree is so upset that she forgets to take in her washing, and it gets rained on during the night.

When the vet comes to see Toby, he says, "Toby is very sick and in pain. He can't get better. It would be kindest to put him to sleep."

"We'll do it tomorrow," says Mom, sadly.

"Good!" says Sara, and she storms up the stairs and won't come down for dinner.

Ben and I pet and hug that smelly old dog. I tell him we'll bury him in the yard with his chewed old tennis balls so that he'll always remember us and our place.

We knock on Sara's door, but she won't answer.

"I hate her," says Ben, and he bangs on the door until Sara shouts at him to leave her alone.

In the middle of the night Ben's crying wakes me. "Put on your robe," I say. "We'll go and stay with Toby until morning."

We switch on the light in the hall and tiptoe down the stairs. But Toby already has company.

I guess Mom was right. Sara does still love Toby, after all.

Toby's buried with the tennis balls in the backyard under the gum tree. Sometimes Ben and I bat a ball to each other, and when it rolls into the bushes, Sara looks up from her book with a small smile and says, very softly, "Fetch, boy, fetch!"